EVERYONE
GETS A
SAY

To all the Someones, may you each get your Say. And to Mom and Dad,
who always let me have mine. —J.T.

For Jill —EG.K.

Everyone Gets a Say • Text copyright © 2020 by Jill Twiss • Illustrations copyright © 2020 by EG Keller • All rights reserved. Printed in the United States of America. • No part of this book may be used or reproduced in any manner whatsoever without written permission except in the case of brief quotations embodied in critical articles and reviews. For information address HarperCollins Children's Books, a division of HarperCollins Publishers, 195 Broadway, New York, NY 10007. • www.harpercollinschildrens.com • Library of Congress Control Number: 2020931650 • ISBN 978-0-06-293375-1 • The artist created the illustrations for this book digitally. Design by Chelsea C. Donaldson • 20 21 22 23 24 PC 10 9 8 7 6 5 4 3 2 1 ❖ First Edition

EVERYONE
GETS A SAY

Written by Jill Twiss   Illustrated by EG Keller

HARPER
An Imprint of HarperCollinsPublishers

Pudding was a quiet snail and did not like Shouting. So when he woke up to the sound of loud BELLOWS and HONKS, he poked his head out of his house . . . which was inside his other house.

Lately it seemed like Pudding's friends couldn't agree on anything. Today they were trying to decide what to plant in a sunny patch of land, and it was *not* going well.

Whatever Toast the butterfly wanted, Jitterbug the chipmunk Did Not.

"Did you know that butterflies drink nectar from flowers using their tongues like straws?" asked Toast. "We should plant flowers!"

"But but but," said Jitterbug. "Acorns grow into trees, and trees will give us EVEN MORE ACORNS."

And whatever Duffles and Nudge the otters wanted, Geezer the goose was Absolutely Against.

"No plants—" shouted Duffles.

"—just mud!" continued Nudge.

"So we can slide big tummy-slides into the lake!" they finished together.

"Honk honk HONK," bellowed Geezer. "I insist on vegetables and I do NOT care to hear what anyone else has to say."

The Yells got louder.

And the Shouts got shoutier.

Pudding had just begun to squish back into his shell when—

DID YOU KNOW THAT BEES HAVE QUEENS?

Everyone got quiet.

"What what what?" asked Jitterbug.

"A Queen Bee is a Someone who leads the bees," said Toast.

"Whoa," said Jitterbug. "Do *we* need a Someone to bring us together?"

"Yes!" said Nudge. "A Someone to be our voice—"

"—when we all have different voices," finished Duffles.

Even Geezer gave a honk of approval.

The friends had finally found something
they all agreed on, until . . .

"But but but," said Jitterbug. "How do we *choose* that Someone?"

"Maybe the Someone who is in charge—" interrupted Nudge.

"—should be the Someone who is the *Tallest*," finished Duffles.

"What if we—" started Pudding, but no one listened.

"Wait wait wait!" exclaimed Jitterbug. "Maybe the Someone who is in charge should be the Someone who is the *Fastest*."

"Huff! Puff! If you would just listen—"

"Honk honk HONK," interrupted Geezer. "The Someone who is in charge should be the Someone who is the LOUDEST!"

HONK!

No matter how hard he tried, Pudding couldn't get anyone to listen to him.

"Wait wait wait!" spluttered Jitterbug.
"Where is Pudding?"

The friends looked everywhere
they could think of.

No Pudding.

Then they heard a tiny *squish*.

"Look look look!" shouted Jitterbug.
"What does that mean?"

EVERYONE GETS A SAY

"That means that you Say who you want to be in charge," said Pudding. "Then I Say who I want to be in charge. And Duffles and Nudge and Geezer and Toast Say who they want to be in charge."

"Whoa," said Jitterbug. "That is a lot lot lot of Saying."

"And after everyone gets their Say, we count. And whichever Someone most of us want to be in charge *is* in charge," added Pudding.

"Honk honk HONK! What about the loudest Someone?" squawked Geezer, even louder than usual.

But Pudding wasn't finished. "When Everyone Gets a Say, the very quietest Someone gets the same Say as the very loudest Someone. The very tiniest Someone gets the same Say as the very biggest Someone."

Pudding stretched up a little taller as he realized that everyone was listening to him now.

"It's called Voting," said Pudding. "Voting is how you have a Say, even when no one will listen to you."

"We think it's—" said Duffles.

"—a great idea!" finished Nudge.

"Honk honk HONK," said Geezer. "Let's all have our Say."

And they did.

"We believe having our Say—" began Nudge.

"—is of Ottermost importance," finished Duffles.

"Honk honk VOTE!" said Geezer.

ONE SOMEONE ONE ACORN

I'M WITH FUR

DUCK DUCK GOOSE

"Hello hello hello! I have a very important announcement to make," said Jitterbug. "The Friends of the Forest have had their Say. And the Someone who shall be in charge is . . ."

PUDDING THE SNAIL!

Pudding was very surprised. He squished forward and spoke quietly. This time everyone was listening.

"Fellow Someones, I promise to listen to every single one of your voices. Because it doesn't matter if you're the tallest or the shortest or the squishiest or the fluffiest or even the quietest . . .

". . . In our Forest, every Someone Gets a Say."